# Snowman's
# Big Job

# For Irene and Maryanna

ISBN 0-439-58392-6

Text copyright © 2004 by Scholastic Inc. Illustrations copyright © 2004 by Janet Kusmierski * All rights reserved. Published by Scholastic Inc. * SCHOLASTIC and associated logos are trademarks and/or registered trademarks of Scholastic Inc.

12 11 10 9 8 7 6 5 4 3 2

4 5 6 7 8 9/0

Printed in the U.S.A.

First printing, December 2004

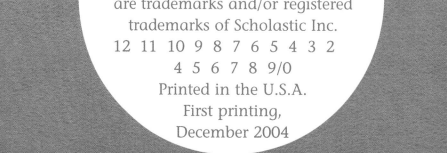

Special thanks to Gina Shaw, Jennifer Rinaldi, Elizabeth Bennett, Cecily Kaiser, and Paul Colin for getting this "Snowman" built. Additional thanks to Ken Geist, Grace Maccarone, and Liz Mills for their expertise.

# Snowman's Big Job

by Janet Kusmierski
words by Elizabeth Bennett

Photos by Paul Colin / Cezanne Studio

## SCHOLASTIC INC.

New York   Toronto   London   Auckland   Sydney
Mexico City   New Delhi   Hong Kong   Buenos Aires

When I grow up,
what will I be?
My snowmen friends
will help me see.

# ONE

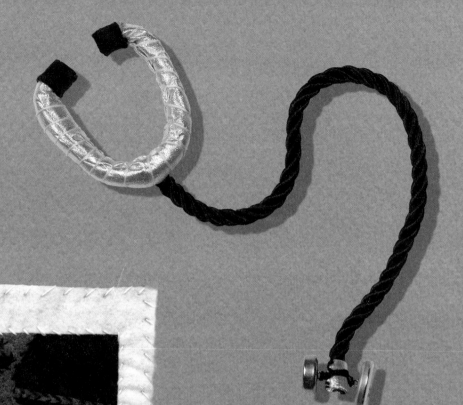

# TWO

# THREE

What will I be?

A doctor!

ONE

TWO

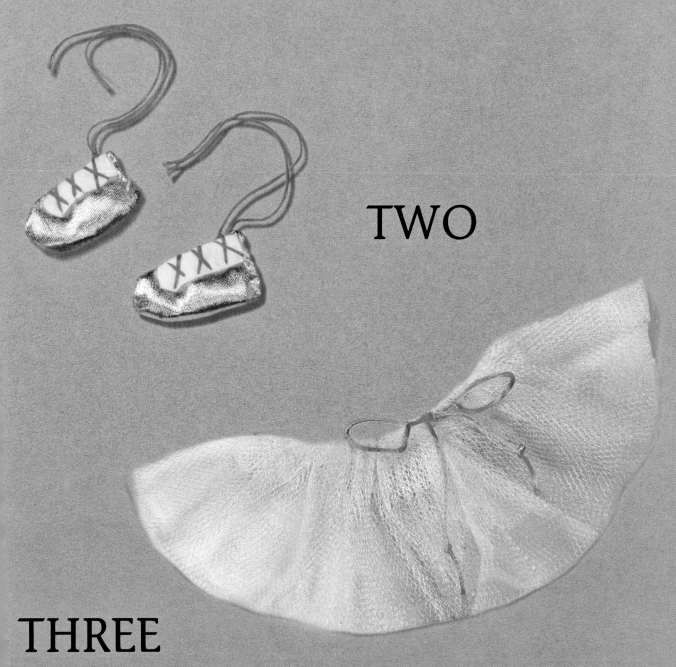

THREE

What will I be?

A ballerina!

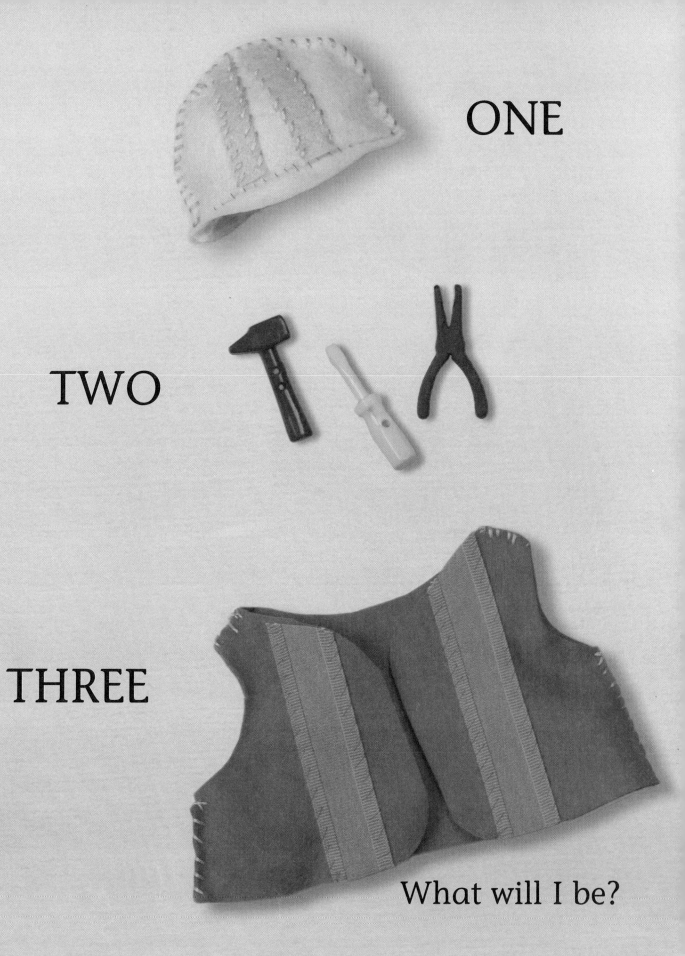

ONE

TWO

THREE

What will I be?

A construction worker!

ONE

TWO

THREE

What will I be?

A chef!

ONE

TWO

THREE

What will I be?

A firefighter!

ONE

TWO

THREE

What will I be?

# An artist!

# ONE

# TWO

# THREE

What will I be?

An astronaut!

ONE

TWO

THREE

What will I be?

# A police officer!

ONE

TWO

THREE

What will I be?

A pilot!

ONE

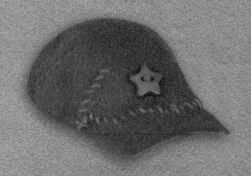

TWO

THREE

What will I be?

# A truck driver!

ONE

TWO

THREE

What will I be?

# A mail carrier!

ONE

TWO

# A B C
# a b c

THREE

What will I be?

A teacher!

ONE

TWO

THREE

What will I be?

# A zookeeper!

I guess I'll have
to wait and see—
which job
will be right for me!